NANCY DREW

Hello, HOLLYWOOD!

by Fern Alexander
based on the screenplay by Tiffany Paulsen
and the characters created by Carolyn Keene

Ready-to-Read

Simon Spotlight

New York   London   Toronto   Sydney

Based on the movie *NANCY DREW* by Warner Bros. Entertainment Inc.

SIMON SPOTLIGHT
An imprint of Simon & Schuster Children's Publishing Division
1230 Avenue of the Americas, New York, New York 10020
NANCY DREW © Warner Bros. Enertainment Inc. NANCY DREW is a trademark of
Simon & Schuster, Inc. (s07)

Manufactured in the United States of America
First Edition
2 4 6 8 10 9 7 5 3 1
Library of Congress Cataloging-in-Publication Data
Alexander, Fern.
Hello, Hollywood! / by Fern Alexander ; based on the screenplay by
Tiffany Paulsen and on the characters created by Carolyn Keene. — 1st ed.
p. cm. — (Ready-to-read)
"Based on the movie Nancy Drew by Warner Bros. Entertainment Inc."
ISBN-13: 978-1-4169-3900-9
ISBN-10: 1-4169-3900-8
I. Paulsen, Tiffany. II. Keene, Carolyn. III. Nancy Drew
(Motion picture) IV. Title.
PZ7.A3769He 2007
2006032337

Nancy was excited. Her dad had a job
in Hollywood, and she was going
with him!

"I will be back in a few months,"
she told her friends.

Nancy's friend Ned gave her
a compass.
"See that arrow?" said Ned.
"It's fixed so that when you are
in Los Angeles, it points
the way back to River Heights."

Nancy could not believe her eyes
when they arrived in Los Angeles.
The city was so busy and noisy!
It was a big change from River Heights.

Nancy's new home was a mansion
once owned by Dehlia Draycott,
a famous movie actress. Dehlia
disappeared twenty-five years ago.

Barbara Barbara, the real-estate agent, told Nancy, "Have a look around the house. There are booby traps all over!"
Nothing could be better than a mansion with a mystery, Nancy thought.

Barbara introduced Nancy to
Mr. Leshing, the caretaker.
"He lives in an apartment
down the hill," she explained.
"Please let me know if there is
anything I can do for you,"
Mr. Leshing told Nancy.

The next morning Nancy headed to
her first day at Hollywood High,
All the girls stared at her.
With her cardigan, handbag,
and spiral-bound notebook,
Nancy looked really out of place!

When she raised her hand to answer
a question in calculus class,
the other kids raised their eyebrows.
"The quadratic formula is negative B
plus or minus the square root of B
squared minus four AC all over two A,"
Nancy said as they snickered.

At lunch she sat next to Trish
in the cafeteria. Trish laughed
when Nancy laid out her napkin
with chicken-salad sandwiches,
carrot sticks, apple slices,
a cupcake, and hot cocoa.
Nancy was definitely not from L.A.!

"I am sitting next to Martha Stewart,"
Trish told her friend Inga, who was
sitting across the table.
"And I am going to take
her cupcake," Trish added.

When Inga and Trish overheard Nancy
telling the principal to offer a CPR
course, they came up with a plan
to play a mean trick on her.

At the basketball game later,
Inga's brother, Corky, pretended
to choke.
"Does anyone know CPR?"
Inga cried out.
Sure enough, Nancy came to help.
She grabbed Corky from behind
and pushed up on his chest. A large
piece of pretzel flew out of his
mouth! But he was still not
breathing. So Nancy placed him
on the floor.
Suddenly Corky opened his eyes.
"You are even cuter close up,"
he told Nancy, as everyone
in the gym laughed.
Nancy could not believe it!

Corky felt bad after Nancy left
the gym. So he went to her house.
"Hi," Corky told Nancy, "I'm sorry
about what happened."
"I have to say I felt a little hurt,"
she said. "But thank you.
You are a gentleman."

Corky tried to find something else
to say. "There is a mystery
to this house," he said.
"Yes, I know," Nancy replied, and she
told him what she had found out.

Later Corky and Nancy were walking
around looking for clues when they
stumbled onto a 1950s movie set.
A famous movie actor was reading
the Miranda rights to a crook.

Nancy shook her head. "Excuse me," she said, "but the reading of the Miranda rights upon arrest was not law until 1966."
The actor was impressed.
"Would you like to direct this film?" he asked Nancy as the director stomped off the set.

Nancy spent the next few days
working on the mystery.
She found out that Dehlia Draycott
had a daughter many years ago.
After knocking on many doors,
Nancy found the long-lost woman,
Jane Brighton. Jane's daughter, Allie,
looked exactly like Dehlia!

"Your mother was Dehlia Draycott,"
Nancy told Jane.
Jane was shocked by the news.

Soon after, Nancy received a special surprise. Ned showed up at her doorstep with her car! He had driven all the way from River Heights.

"Happy almost your birthday!" he said.

Nancy thought it would be fun
to celebrate her birthday in Hollywood
with a party. She handed out invitations
at school.

Dear Friend,
You are cordially invited to attend a birthday party for Nancy Drew. Eight p.m., Saturday evening. Appropriate dress, please. I hope you attend,
Nancy.

And even though they thought Nancy was weird, Trish and Inga decided to go to the party.

On the night of the party Nancy's
house quickly filled up with
people and loud music.
Ned brought out a cake and tried
his best to sing, "Happy birthday"–
when someone came crashing
down on it!

All of a sudden Inga yelled out,
"Trish can't breathe! This is
not a joke!"
Everyone made way for Nancy as she
tried to help Trish. Nancy's CPR
training worked–and Trish opened
her eyes!

"I have to admit I thought you were
an insane person before, but
you are not," Inga told Nancy.
"You are terrific."

To thank her for saving Trish's life,
Inga took Nancy shopping for clothes.
But the owner of the store liked
what Nancy was already wearing.

"It is just darling," she said.
"I have to take pictures! Have you
    made other pieces?"

Nancy happily showed off her clothes
as Inga rolled her eyes.
There was nothing Nancy could not do!

Over the next few days
Nancy helped find the will
that said Dehlia had left
her mansion to Jane.

Jane also found out that
Mr. Leshing was her father!
Nancy was happy that she had
solved another case—and just
in time, too. She and her dad
were about to return
to River Heights.

Hollywood had been an adventure, Nancy thought. But she really looked forward to returning to her friends—especially Ned!